# PHILOSOPHY OF LIFE
# STORIES FOR
# YOUNG PEOPLE

KENNETH E. POLLOCK

# PHILOSOPHY OF LIFE
# STORIES FOR
# YOUNG PEOPLE

## Volume One

Illustrations by Willard Whitlock

Isis Publishing House, Ltd.
New York, NY

Second Printing 2007

This edition is published by Isis Publishing House, Ltd.,
New York City

Library of Congress Control Number: 2006922682

Pollock, Kenneth E.
Philosophy of life—stories for young people
volume one/Kenneth E. Pollock
ISBN 0-9662281-1-1
YBBG # 0359

Isis Publishing House Ltd.,
4620 Kings Highway
P.O. Box 340487
Brooklyn, New York 11234-0487

Edited by Patricia Boothe/Ivor Baker
Editorial Consultants: Dorothy Pelzer Brown/Desmond Campbell
Illustrations: Willard Whitlock
Art Consultant: Chinwe Ifeoma
Cover Design: Luanda Lozano / Lozano Design

---

ATTENTION ORGANIZATIONS, SCHOOLS AND INDIVIDUALS:
Quantity discounts are available on bulk purchases of this book for educational or
fundraising purposes. For information, contact
Isis Publishing House, Ltd.
4620 Kings Highway, P.O. Box 340487, Brooklyn, New York 11234-0487
Telephone: (212) 882-1018 • (718) 253-9387 • Fax: (718) 253-2699
e-mail: isispublishingco@aol.com
website: www.isispublishingusa.com

PRINTED AND BOUND IN THE UNITED STATES OF AMERICA BY
CONQUERING BOOKS, LLC
210 E. Arrowhead Dr. #01
Charlotte, NC 28213
www.conqueringbooks.com
Tel: (704) 509-2226

# ADVANCE ACCLAIM FOR
## PHILOSOPHY OF LIFE
## STORIES FOR YOUNG PEOPLE

The educational philosophy of Medgar Evers College of the City University of New York is rooted in the belief that education is the most effective way to transform lives. **Philosophy of Life—Stories for Young People** incorporates this philosophy into a collection of short stories painted in shades of life. This book reflects our shared commitment to ensure the emergence of this generation's adolescent community into the future leaders and entrepreneurs of our City.

Realizing the importance of educational initiatives that encourage and equip adolescents with the moral and ethical values needed to accomplish success, your book is a welcomed contribution to the education of children of African descent, especially those in urban settings.

*Dr. Edison O. Jackson, President, Medgar Evers College, Brooklyn, NY*

Ken Pollock is a modern day Aesop whose **Philosophy of Life—Stories for Young People** brings the values and attitudes that we want to see in our world...

*Dr. Winsome Miller-Rowe M.B.B.S., F.A.A.P, Pediatrician,*
*Musicologist, Music/Video Producer, Jamaica, West Indies*

Mr. Pollock, this writing is great! I have not seen anything like **Philosophy of Life—Stories for Young People** since Aesop's Fables. I am certainly going to recommend this book to my church, family and friends.

*Sylvia Schultz, Harlem, NY*

Keep up the good work in the interest of the youths of our nation.

*McCartha Rose Lewis*

An excellent book by a thoughtful author...

*Oliver Samuels, O.D., Actor*

**Philosophy of Life—Stories for Young People** is a book that schools and churches worldwide must have in their instructional or supplemental learning programs. The content is extraordinarily academic, philosophical and streetwise in nature...

*Dr. Eric Brown, CEO, Hilton Vaughn Foundation, Former Faculty, Columbia*
*University, NYC/Joy T. Vaughn, Author: Three Mean Alligator Project*

I would recommend this book to anyone who wants to learn about life in a positive way.

*Kevin J. Clark, MS, Educational Therapist*

...This book is an effective tool for teaching good morals—virtues that are so much needed today...

*S. Reginald Michael, PhD*

...I have read and am fascinated by Volume One of Mr. Pollock's **Philosophy of Life—Stories for Young People...** I like it so much that I have, just for the moment, imagined that I could turn back the clock of my own life...

*Honorable Percy Ellis Sutton*
*Chairman, Inner City Broadcasting Corporation, NYC*

...Material of this genre should be included in literature to which high school students are exposed, particularly so if their parents originate in the Antilles and their progeny tend, in embracing the urges of the North American milieu, to forget their roots...

*William F. Dore, MBE, Educator,*
*Retired Chief Education Officer, St. Kitts & Nevis*

Mr. Pollock writes the way it sounds, for today's children.

*Leona Sanders, Grandmother, Staten Island, NY*

Children all over the world, from tiny villages and hamlets, to cities, must be given an opportunity to read Ken Pollock's prose...

*Herman Hall, Publisher, EVERYBODY'S Caribbean Magazine*

...This is a book worth having and I recommend it to teachers, parents and young people, in particular, and everyone else, in general. This book bears some similarities with the book of Proverbs in the Bible, in that all of the wisdom stories end with an appropriate treasured moral...

*Dr. Alanzo H. Smith, Counseling Psychologist, Family Ministries*
*Director, Greater New York Conference of SDA,*
*Author:* **When Loving You Is Destroying Me**

This book represents a powerful tool for educating our children and helping them develop the skills they will need to become responsible, productive members of our community.

*Howard Golden, Former President of the Borough of Brooklyn*

The depth of culture is the foundation for our children's future.

As a tool for educators, the writings and characters represent the best in us as ethical people...

*Richard E. Green, MA, Educator and Chief Executive of the Collective*
*Fellowship & Peace Academy, Author:* **Tags, Ups & Ancient Jewels**

To My Children:

David Kwame Rameses
Charisse Cleopatra Isis
Denise Nefertiti Nandi
Patrice Roshan Nkrumah

And My Grandchildren:

Jahde Makeba Pollock
Story Koryn Young
Sydney Jae'La Pollock
Shania Ashley Pollock
Mekhi Kenyetta Pollock

Thanks to Allison B. Brito of Cornerstone Creations and Publications for her editing and graphic design consultation.

# PREFACE

The stories in **Philosophy of Life—Stories for Young People** can be appreciated and cherished by all, regardless of age. The stories allow older readers to reflect on similar stories they read in their youth. They will find stories similar to the hare and the tortoise, which teaches the virtue of patience and intelligence; the antics of a spider (Brer Anancy), which is recognized as an Ashanti spider-god who is endowed with magical powers to become whatever he chooses; and "Brer Rabbit," a crafty and sinister trickster, who uses wits and wisdom to get out of trouble.

The use of animals in the stories will not only titillate and entertain our young readers but will also serve as teaching tools, to motivate and inspire them to learn the true lessons of life. The aim of the book is to impart the principles of morality, self-esteem and loyalty through stories that show how positive and negative behaviors and attitudes can impact our lives.

**Philosophy of Life—Stories for Young People** is rendered in three parts: Volume One for children eight to twelve years old, Volume Two for children thirteen to eighteen years old, and Volume Three for adults.

The stories in each book are intended to instill self-esteem, mentoring and leadership skills in young people. The reader can identify with aspects of the character's personality and apply what was learned to daily life. Patience, sacrifice, faith, conflict resolution, goal setting, understanding, tolerance, good planning, hope, courage, independence and respect for others are some of the principles taught.

K.E.P.

# ACKNOWLEDGMENTS

## I am blessed and grateful!

I would like to acknowledge the tremendous support, assistance and guidance given to me while writing this book by family, special friends and associates. My sincere appreciation to my wife, Yvonne Humphrey, for bringing into my life a higher level of spiritual consciousness, which has catapulted me on to greater things, and to my four children, David, Charisse, Denise and Patrice, for their endearing support over the years.

I am indebted to Mamadou Chinyelu for providing valued consultation and assistance in the establishment of my publishing company and to Patricia Boothe (PBOO WORKS) for editing, formatting and providing insightful advice and technical expertise. I am also grateful to Lisa Teamer and Willard Whitlock for their artistic creativity and contributions. I also owe a debt of gratitude to the staff of Far Better Printing & Copy Center and Flatbush Copy Center for their generous assistance throughout the writing of my manuscript.

I am also indebted to Percy Sutton, the chairman emeritus of Innercity Broadcasting Corporation, for providing media time and his staff for encouraging me to publish my ideas, and also to Herman Hall of Everybody's Magazine for publishing my first article encouraging African-Americans to participate in the U.S. presidential elections of 1976.

I wish also to express my gratitude to John Henrik Clarke, Dr. Marco Mason, Willis Cheatham, Dr. Carlos Russell, David Lampell, Walter Edwards and George A. McMillan for believing in my creative abilities, taking the time to recommend resource books and returning my many telephone calls. Special thanks to Marian Gayle, Neville Bushell and Karl Carr for their continuing support.

There are also several family members who have influenced me greatly. My late grandmother, Anna Rowe, a spiritualist and activist, who became an ancestor at the age of 90, was a beautiful African descendant. She, together with my aunt, Florence Nelson, and my late mother, Edith Nelson, are the rocks that helped to build the foundation on which I stand today. My heartfelt thanks also to the staff, family members and especially the children of Amboy Neighborhood Center, Harriet Tubman Family Center, Harlem Dowling Center and the Ruth Hernandez Center.

**THANK YOU ALL!**

# TABLE OF CONTENTS

The youth gets together his materials to build a bridge to the moon, or perchance, a palace or temple on the earth, and, at length, the middle-aged man concludes to build a woodshed with them.

*—Henry Thoreau*
*Journal, July 14, 1852*

# THE SNAKE AND THE LIZARDS

One day, after a rainstorm, two lizards sat on a limb on the top of a tree drying themselves in the sun.

They noticed a snake on the ground below the tree, wiggling its way through the leaves and puddles of water.

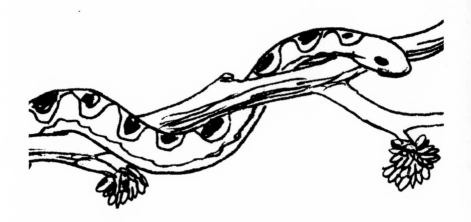

"Say, Mister Snake, where are you going in such a hurry?" yelled one of the lizards to the snake.

"I am trying to get to a tree so I, too, can find a dry, sunny spot for myself to recover from the rain," the snake responded, as it reached the bottom of the tree.

"You have the whole ground to make your home. Why do you have to come to this tree for shelter?" the other lizard asked.

Both lizards laughed.

"You should be the last one to laugh," said the snake. "There you are, living at the top of a tree, without enough sense to build a roof to protect yourselves from the rain and from predators. How can you, tell me, about my house on the ground, where the water settles?" the snake said, as he slithered up the tree and settled on a dry branch.

The lizards were so busy laughing, they did not see an eagle circling nearby. The eagle swooped down from the sky, snatched one of the lizards and the other lizard fell to the ground.

## MORAL

*Be sure your own house is in order*
*before giving advice to others.*

# THE CRAB AND THE TURTLE

**A** land turtle and a land crab were out hunting for their meal when they noticed an object in the distance. The crab, being faster, reached the object first and discovered it was an almond nut. The crab tried breaking the shell of the almond nut, but realized its claws were not strong enough.

When the turtle arrived, it picked up the almond nut in its powerful jaws, cracked the shell, and proceeded to eat the nut.

"What about me? I deserve a half of that nut," cried the crab. "I reached it first."

"When you reached the nut first and tried to break the shell, were you planning to give me a half of it?" asked the turtle. "I am sure that if you were strong enough to break the shell, you would have eaten the nut!"

## **MORAL**

*Do to others as you would like them to do to you.*

# THE TWO ANTS AND THE BREAD CRUMB

**A** black ant and a red ant were out seeking food when they both saw a crumb of bread on the kitchen floor. They ran to the crumb and began pulling on opposite ends. After several minutes of pulling the crumb back and forth, neither would give in to the other.

Finally, the black ant said, "We are not getting anywhere like this. Let us share the crumb so we can both be happy."

"That is a good idea," the red ant said, "but how are we going to share?"

"We are going to divide the crumb in two equal parts," the black ant responded.

"Oh no, we cannot," said the red ant, "for my family is larger than yours. I have more mouths to feed; therefore, I should get the larger portion."

"Your family may be larger than mine, but we found this crumb of bread, not your family. I am afraid you just have to keep on hunting until you find more food," said the black ant.

The black ant took half of the crumb and ran back into its hole.

## **MORAL**

*Equal work, equal pay.*

# THE STOVE AND THE REFRIGERATOR

**A** stove, unhappy with its condition, complained to the refrigerator: "If I were like you, I would retain the same temperature all day. Instead, I go from cold, to hot, to warm, and back to cold again."

The refrigerator responded, "At least we are being

used. When the time comes that we are no longer being used, then I will become concerned."

The owner of the house entered the kitchen, looked at an old pot on the stove and said to his wife, "The next time we go shopping, we have to replace that pot. It has seen the last of its days." The owner then removed the pot from the stove and placed it next to the garbage pail.

On seeing this, the stove said to the refrigerator, "Please forgive me for my foolish statement."

The refrigerator simply responded, "You are forgiven."

---

## **<u>MORAL</u>**

*When you give thanks for little things,*
*big things come your way.*

---

# THE SELFISH SPIDER

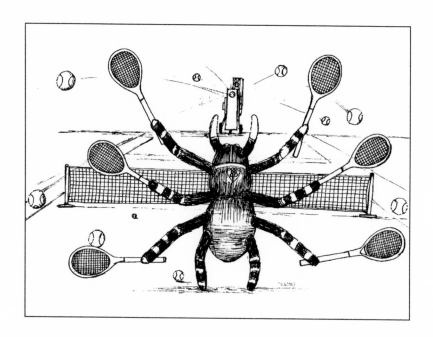

**A** mother spider turned to her son and asked, "Why don't you play tennis anymore? You have not played for weeks!"

"I cannot find anyone to play with me," responded the son.

"I thought you and the rabbit were good friends. You seem to get along well with him," the mother spider said.

"The rabbit says I am always winning. I think he is jealous of me," said the son.

"It is fair that since you are a better player than he is, you should win? That does not mean you cannot encourage him by letting him win one or two games. It is very selfish of you not to let him win sometimes," the mother spider replied.

"But I cannot lose. You always tell me to be good and to be the best at whatever I do," said the son.

"I told you to be the best, but I did not teach you to be selfish. In a game, as in life, you cannot survive alone; you have to learn to share and care. You have to share the losses as well as the gains. If you do not, you will soon have no friends," the mother spider advised her son.

"I think I am beginning to lose friends already," said the son. "The rabbit has refused to play with me."

## **MORAL**

*Sometimes we can expect to lose a little,*
*in order to gain more in life.*

# THE GOAT AND THE FROG

One hot, sunny day, an old ram goat was out grazing in the fields. It became very thirsty and decided to search for water. The goat searched and searched until it found a running stream, but the bank of the stream was too steep for the goat to climb.

The goat walked along the bank of the stream until it found a place low enough to climb over, but the area was muddy and soft.

"I may get stuck and not be able to get out," the goat said to itself.

The goat continued to walk along the bank before coming to another low area. The soil there was solid, but there were thickets, thorns and dry plants blocking the path. Using its horns and hooves, the goat started clearing a path to get through. As the goat cleared the path, it noticed some live thorns between the dry thorns and the water's edge.

"I will not be able to get through those thorns," the goat pondered.

The goat was about to turn away in disappointment when suddenly a frog appeared on a water lily, drying itself in the sun.

"Let me see how I can trick this frog into helping," the goat thought to itself.

Calling out to the frog, the goat said, "Oh, Froggy, you must be tired from jumping all day."

"Not really. Jumping is my way of getting from one place to another," the frog responded.

"How high can you jump?" the goat asked.

"About six to ten feet," the frog said.

"How far can you jump?" the goat inquired.

"About fifteen to twenty feet," the frog replied, extending its tongue to catch a flying insect.

"My, my," the goat said, "I'm always amazed by the swiftness of frogs in using their tongues. How long is your tongue?" the goat asked.

"About twelve to fifteen inches when fully extended," the frog replied.

"How much water do you drink daily?" the goat asked.

"Well, I live in ponds, on rocks and water lilies. The water is my home," the frog responded.

"How far can you spit?" asked the goat.

The frog suddenly realized what the goat was up to.

"What are you trying to get me to do?" asked the frog.

"Well, I am very thirsty and badly in need of some water to drink. I thought I would ask you to give me some water," the goat said, hanging its head in shame.

"You did not ask. You were trying to trick me!" said the frog angrily. "If you had told me that your path was blocked and you could not reach the water, I would have gladly assisted you. I would have shown you how to bypass the thicket, thorns and dry plants," the frog said.

"Instead, you gave me the impression you cared about me by the questions you asked. In doing so, you were simply looking out for yourself. I would have told you how to get water if you simply asked."

Having said that, the frog jumped into the pond and disappeared, leaving the goat still standing there with its problem unsolved.

A small herd of cattle suddenly appeared, led by a bull and a few cows with their calves. Startled, the goat left the edge of the pond in a hurry without getting the water it needed.

## **MORAL**

*Honesty is the best policy.*

# THE LIZARD AND THE FROG

One day, a frog waited on the curb of a busy highway to cross over to the other side. It then noticed a lizard nearby, panting in the hot sun.

"Where are you going?" asked the frog.

"I am trying to cross this highway to get to those tall, shady trees where it is cooler," the lizard responded.

"So why don't you cross? What are you waiting for?" asked the frog.

"I have two things working against me, the busy traffic and the heat. It is more than one hundred degrees on the hot street. I think it is too risky for me," said the lizard.

"So what are you going to do? Stand here all day?" asked the frog.

"No. I was hoping you would allow me to climb onto your back when you jump across the street, so I can get there safely," said the lizard.

"Why should I carry you on my back? That would weaken my jump, risk two lives instead of one and increase my chance of not making it across. The same dangers you anticipate are also of concern to me but, in spite of them, I do what is necessary. You cannot enjoy the comfort of those cool trees unless you take the risk of crossing the street," advised the frog.

The frog made two leaps and crossed the road, leaving the lizard behind.

## **<u>MORAL</u>**

*In life you have to take chances.*

# THE FARMER, THE DOG
# AND THE CAT

**A** cat that was jealous of the relationship between its master and its master's dog decided to turn the master against the dog.

The master's wife baked a golden brown meat loaf and placed it in a dish on the kitchen counter to cool. The meat loaf would be served for the family's dinner later that evening.

When she left the kitchen, the cat ate the meat loaf and disappeared to another room in the house.

When the master's wife returned to the kitchen, she noticed that the dish was empty. The dog was lying in its usual spot on a mat at the entrance to the kitchen. Believing that the dog was guilty, she yelled at it, and chased it from the room.

When the master returned home, she told him that the dog had eaten the meat loaf. The master summoned the dog and scolded it, but the dog denied stealing the meat loaf.

A few days later, the cat ate a plate of fried chicken and placed the bones in a corner where the master's

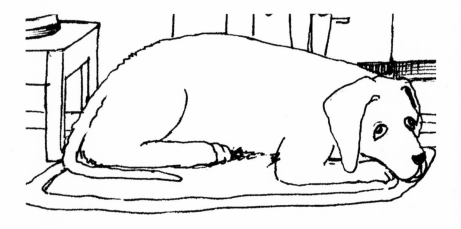

wife would find them. When she told her husband about this, he immediately suspected that the cat was the thief. The master knew that if the dog had eaten the fried chicken he would also have eaten the bones.

The master summoned the cat.

"I am taking you to the doctor," he said.

"Why?" asked the cat.

"You look swollen. I feed you the same portion every day, but you seem to be getting bigger! Obviously, something must be wrong. I hope you are not seriously ill, because you may need surgery or even to be put to sleep," said the master to the cat.

The cat immediately confessed. The cat told its master that it stole the food because it was jealous of the dog, and knew the dog would be blamed for stealing the food.

---

## **MORAL**

*Jealousy can change people into liars and thieves.*

---

# THE FARMER AND THE CAT

Early one morning, a cat entered its master's house with the remains of a dead lizard in its mouth.  The cat's master—a farmer—chased the cat out of the house and into the yard.

In its rush to get away, the cat spilled a fresh bucket of milk the farmer had just taken from a cow. The farmer became angry and gave the cat away.

In a few days, mice and rats took over the house. The farmer, frustrated at this, said to himself, "A bucket of milk is a very small price to pay; I have been a terrible fool."

The farmer retrieved the cat, and when he brought it home said, "Do whatever you want to make yourself comfortable in this house."

Within a few days, all the mice and rats were gone, and the master was once again very happy with his cat.

## __MORAL__

*We need to think before we act.*

# A BASKET OF BREAD

Each morning, a teenage boy assisted his father, the baker, by delivering bread to the villagers before going to school. The father went to the bakery at four o'clock every morning to bake bread, and the son arrived two hours later to begin his delivery.

One morning, the son overslept, so he had less time to complete his deliveries before going to school. While the boy rushed to make his deliveries, a loaf of bread fell from the basket he carried on his head, and rolled down a hill.

The boy removed the basket from his head, placed it on the side of the road, and ran after the single loaf. He chased the loaf of bread all the way to the bottom of the hill, where he found it floating away in a creek.

The boy climbed back up the hill to the place where he had left his basket and found it surrounded by a pack of dogs. When he chased the dogs away, all that remained in the basket were crumbs of bread.

---

## **MORAL**

*Often, people who go through life worrying about what they have lost, and not giving thanks for what they still have, lose their remaining possessions due to neglect.*

---

# THE BEAR AND THE GORILLA

Once upon a time, a group of animals gathered in the forest to discuss their various skills.

The elephant demonstrated how it used its tusk to take the bark from trees for its meals. It also made a mighty sound to demonstrate how it scared off its enemies.

The lion showed how it used its powerful paws to kill its enemies with one blow.

The chameleon lizard showed how it changed color to blend with its surroundings so that it could escape from its predators or catch its victims.

The skunk, not to be outdone, sprayed its fluid with its horrible smell to show how it defended itself.

Several other animals and insects demonstrated their skills as well.

The polar bear and the silver-back gorilla were the last to demonstrate their capabilities. Both agreed that because of their huge size, they could survive anywhere, even outside of their own habitats. The polar bear said it could survive in the deepest and hottest part of the jungle.

The gorilla said it could survive even in the coldest regions of the North Pole.

So the polar bear and the silver-back gorilla decided to change places. They said goodbye to all the other animals and departed to their new environments.

During the first few days, the polar bear and gorilla were happy to meet new friends and roam their new territories but this did not last long.

As each day passed by, both realized how difficult it was to adapt to a new home. In their own habitats, certain things were understood. Their size and strength gave them the power and authority to do what they wanted. However, in their adopted environments, it was not so easy to maintain their diets.

The gorilla and the polar bear grew weaker and thinner. In time, they would starve to death.

After a few weeks, they returned to the meeting place where the animals had gathered again. The polar bear and the gorilla explained to the others that they wanted to go back to their original homes.

"Why?" the elephant asked.

"I have come to realize that we all have special gifts regardless of our differences in appearance. We are here to make separate contributions," the polar bear responded.

"Yes, we are all creatures of the world, placed here by the same creator. We all use different methods of survival, depending on our habitats. Some of our behaviors may seem strange, cruel and barbaric to others, but we need to accept each other's way of life," said the gorilla.

"I hope both of you have learned your lesson," the wise elephant said to them, sternly. "No one should try to change the plans of nature."

## MORAL

*Each living being is in this world for*
*a special purpose.*

# THE VAIN PARROT

Deep in the forest lived a flock of birds. There were at least one hundred different species of birds. The prettiest of all was a parrot. Its colors made it very noticeable.

On awakening each morning, the parrot would go to the highest branch so all the other birds could watch as it admired itself all day. When the other birds spoke to the parrot, the parrot would respond without looking at them. When the younger birds asked the parrot for advice about survival skills, it ignored them completely.

The parrot did not participate in any organized events and would not watch the baby birds when asked to do so by their parents. It could not be found seeking food, or going to the lake with the other birds for daily baths to get relief from the hot sun.

It remained on its branch all day grooming itself until it was hungry. For meals, it stole from the younger birds and returned to its favorite spot.

One day, while the adult birds were out searching for food, some hunters, who had been watching the parrot for weeks, came to the bird sanctuary. As the younger birds flew away, they yelled out a warning to the parrot, but it ignored them as usual.

The hunters trapped the parrot and put it into a cage, where it spent the rest of its life in captivity.

---

## **MORAL**

*Physical appearance is a small fraction*
*of a beautiful person.*

---

# THE ELEPHANT AND THE MONKEY

One day, a herd of elephants was traveling in search of food and water. After several hours, they came to a high fence made of rocks, which stretched for many miles.

The fence was too steep for the elephants to climb over. The leader of the herd, a large male elephant, gathered them together and said, "We will have to walk alongside the fence until we find a place low enough to climb over."

It summoned the older females of the herd to assist in protecting the baby elephants, and said to them, "Each of you, keep a baby elephant at your side and assist it in keeping up with the adults. We don't know how much longer we will have to travel, but we will assist the young and the weak for as long as our journey lasts." It then ordered them to continue on the journey.

A monkey in a nearby tree, who observed the elephants' dilemma, decided to capitalize on it.

The monkey yelled to the leader, with a noticeable grin on its face, "Say, mister elephant, if I show you how you can cross the fence, what will you give me?"

"What do you want?" the lead elephant responded angrily, already suspicious of the monkey's offer of assistance.

"You see that bunch of ripe bananas over there?" the monkey asked, pointing to a banana tree at a

distance. "If you can pick it for me, I will show you how you can cross over the fence."

"Why don't you pick it for yourself? Aren't you afraid that I will keep it?"

"Do not be foolish," the monkey responded, almost losing its temper. Then it continued with a giggle: "I considered picking it myself, but the banana tree is surrounded by thorns and thicket, and there are no trees nearby for me to swing from to reach it."

The elephant followed the monkey's directions to the banana tree and picked the bunch of bananas. However, instead of giving the bananas to the monkey, the elephant placed them in the thicket, and covered them with thorns.

The monkey's excitement turned to gloom when it saw what the elephant had done with the bananas. "What are you doing? You are supposed to give me the bananas, not bury them!" the monkey said, angrily.

"I have done half of what you requested. Now, please show me how my family and I can cross over. I will give you the bananas then, and we will continue on our journey."

The monkey could not come up with its half of the bargain. It really did not know how the elephants could cross over the fence. All it wanted was the bananas and thought trickery was a good way to get them.

The elephant took the bananas for its family and itself, and said to the monkey, "Thank you. You did not help me cross the fence, but you helped me to feed my family by directing me to the bananas. By the way, there is another bunch of bananas that I picked and covered up with leaves. However, they are green and will take a few days to ripen."

The elephant showed the monkey where the bananas were covered up, summoned its family, and they continued on their journey along the fence.

They crossed over a hill and, less than a mile away, found a place where a windstorm had uprooted a large tree. The tree had fallen on the fence and made a space wide enough for the elephants to cross over.

---

## **<u>MORAL</u>**

*When people are not honest and kind to you,*
*still be honest and kind to them;*
*but move along as soon as you can.*

---

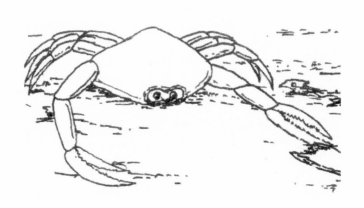

# THE LAND CRAB AND THE SEA CRAB

**A** sea crab found a piece of a fish that fell from the beak of a seagull. It ate some of the fish and gave what was left to a land crab to hold for later.

The land crab became hungry and ate the piece of fish.

When the sea crab returned for the fish, both the land crab and the piece of fish were gone.

## MORAL

*A relative is not always trustworthy.*

# THE RABBIT AND THE SQUIRREL

One day, a rabbit found a nut that it attempted to crack with its teeth. It had no success in doing this, so it tried cracking the nut on a nearby rock. The shell would not break.

The rabbit turned to a squirrel that was close by and asked it to help crack the shell.

The squirrel, having stronger teeth than the rabbit, placed the nut in its mouth, cracked and spit out the shell then ate the nut.

"Where is my nut?" asked the rabbit.

"You did not ask me to give you the nut; you asked me to crack the shell, so I gave you the cracked shell and kept the nut for myself," replied the squirrel.

## MORAL

*When you ask for favors from those who are stronger than yourself, be certain that they are also honest.*

# THE ELEPHANT AND THE HONEYBEE

An elephant that was desperate for food was peeling the bark off a tree when a honeybee landed on the tip of its trunk.

The honeybee pleaded with the elephant to stop peeling the bark from the tree.

"If you peel off the bark, the tree will die and the leaves will fall off and expose the beehive to enemies."

The elephant listened to the plea of the honeybee and moved on to another tree.

The honeybee thanked the elephant and added: "One of these days, I may be able to do a favor for you."

"How can a little insect like you do a favor for a large animal like me?" the elephant smirked.

A few days later, as the honeybee was buzzing about, it heard a moaning sound in the bushes. Following the direction of the sound, it found the elephant wounded and bleeding. The elephant had been shot by a hunter but was able to run away with minor injuries.

The honeybee summoned its family, a swarm of bees that numbered in the tens of thousands. They flew to a nearby pond, and each honeybee carried a drop of water to the elephant and washed away the blood from its wound.

They made another trip to the pond, and brought

back mud, which they dropped into the elephant's wound.

For three days the honeybees brought honey for food to the elephant and protected it from the predators that stood by waiting to attack.

Slowly, the elephant recovered and was soon able to stand on its feet. It thanked the honeybee and wandered into the jungle, happy that its life had been saved, but feeling guilty because it had underestimated the value of the honeybee.

## **MORAL**

*Never judge a person by his or her size.*
*As an individual one may be weak but*
*when organized and united,*
*he or she can become big and strong.*

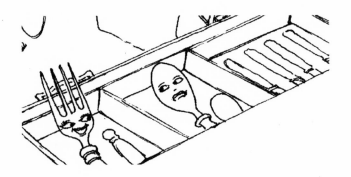

# THE SPOON AND THE FORK

One evening, a spoon said to a fork, as they both lay in the kitchen drawer, "I am happy to have a solid form; it must be a terrible feeling having all those spaces running through you."

"I am happy with my separate fingers. Your purpose is to serve liquid foods, while my purpose is to serve solid foods," said the fork.

"Not only do I serve liquid dishes, but I'm also used to stir tea and lemonade. What else are you good for?" inquired the spoon.

Suddenly, a burglar entered the kitchen with the intention to steal silverware from the drawers. The kitchen was dark, and, as the burglar rummaged through the drawer containing the fork and spoon, the fork pricked him as hard as it could.

The burglar, not knowing what had hurt him, dropped his bag. The bag made a loud clanging sound and woke up the family who had been sleeping upstairs.

The burglar, holding his hand and crying in pain, ran through the door and down the street until he was out of sight.

The fork turned to the spoon and said, "I am also good at defending myself and others against evil. What about you?"

---

## **MORAL**

*Looks can be deceiving.*

---

# THE SMALLEST BOY SCOUT

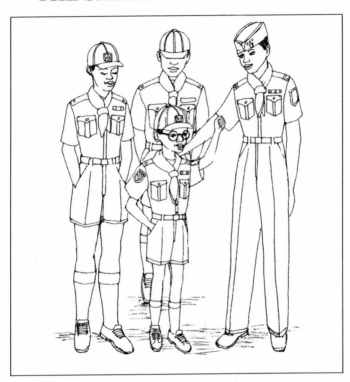

One morning, a group of boy scouts met to start their weekly hike. They waited for an hour for the team leader. When he did not show up, the scoutmaster made an announcement: "It seems that our team leader is delayed this morning. We need to choose a temporary leader for today. Do I have any volunteers?" he asked.

The boys looked at each other, but none of them raised their hand. Finally, the smallest boy in the group stepped forward.

The scoutmaster acknowledged him, saying, "Good, we have a team leader; now we can go."

"He is too small to be a team leader," one boy said.

"He is wearing glasses," another boy said.

"I do not have to be big nor do I have to remove my glasses to be a team leader. I am smart enough to be anything I want to be. And my daddy says I am a born leader," the new team leader replied.

"It takes a great deal of courage and confidence to stand up for yourself like that," the scoutmaster said. "I am proud of you."

The other boys applauded, showing that they accepted him as their leader.

"Okay, scouts. Let's break it up. Everybody, take up your backpacks, line up and follow me," the scoutmaster commanded.

The scouts did as they were ordered.

---

## **MORAL**

*When you believe in yourself,*
*others will trust in you.*

---

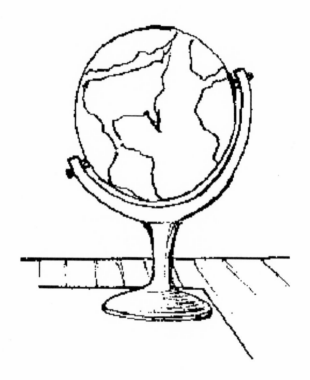

# THE WORLD IS LIKE A PIE

A geography teacher asked her ninth grade class to describe the world for her.

One boy said, "The world is like a large ball that keeps turning and turning."

Another boy raised his hand and said, "A great writer said that the world is a great stage, and we humans are all actors and actresses."

A girl raised her hand and said, "My mother says the world is like a large pie, and the more education we receive, the more we increase our opportunity for a larger portion of the pie."

The teacher awarded her an "A" for her response.

---

## **MORAL**

*The more knowledge you receive, the greater the opportunity for success later in life.*

---

# AFTER SCHOOL FIGHT

One afternoon after school, a group of students was walking home when two boys got into a heated argument. The argument soon turned into a fistfight.

The other children cheered and urged them on to fight.

A young man who was passing by stepped between the two boys and said, "Whatever your differences are, you need to talk it out. You do not have to fight each other."

"He hit me first," said the boy with the bloody nose.

"That's not true," said the boy with the bloody lips.

"I hit him because he called me names," said the boy with the bloody nose.

"So what if he called you names," said the young man who was attempting to stop the fight. "There's a saying, *"Sticks and stones can break my bones, but words can do no harm to me."* You are not judged by the names others call you, but by your response to name-calling. You must be tolerant and try to solve conflicts without fighting each other."

Realizing that he had the attention of all the children, the young man asked the bystanders, "Why didn't you try to stop the fight?"

"I didn't want to get involved," replied one boy.

"I don't know them that well. My family just moved to this neighborhood," said a girl.

"It was none of my business," said another boy.

"I understand your explanations," replied the young man, "but fighting is not the way to settle differences. As you get older, you will be faced with conflicts in your daily lives, and how you choose to deal with those conflicts will show your worth. I hope that in the future when you see your peers arguing, you will try to stop them. You will feel good and have a clear conscience, knowing you cared enough to help."

The young man then turned to the two boys who had been fighting and said, "As for the two of you, I am happy you had no weapons. If you did, the results would have been different." He then asked the boy with the bloodied lips, "Are you an animal?"

"No, I am not," the boy answered.

"Are you a fool?" the young man asked the boy with the bloody nose.

"No," he answered.

"Only animals and fools fight. Physical fighting is a cowardly act; brave people settle their arguments with words," the young man added. "Now, please shake hands and promise never to fight again." The boys shook hands.

The young man turned to the group of children and said, "You should not encourage people to fight since no one wins when fighting. Fighting is always wrong."

When he was satisfied that the boys had calmed down, the young man left and the children continued on their journey home.

---

## **MORAL**

*Cowards fight while the brave discuss their differences.*

---

# THE LOST WALLET

One afternoon, after school, as two teenage boys were walking their regular route home, they saw an old lady stumble and fall.

One boy ran to assist the lady, while yelling to his friend, "Come on and give me a hand! Help me get her on her feet."

"Oh no, not me," the younger boy responded, as he stood by and watched his friend struggling to get the old lady on her feet.

The old lady thanked the older boy and continued on her journey.

"Why did you refuse to help me?" the older boy asked his friend.

"I did not know her!" his young friend exclaimed.

"That's true, neither of us knew her, but that could have been our mother or grandmother lying on the ground," said the older boy as he picked up his schoolbag, and they continued their walk home.

A few days later, as they walked the same route home, they came upon a wallet lying on the curb. The older boy who had assisted the old lady picked up the wallet which  contained a few hundred dollars, an identification card and other personal documents.

"Let us keep the money and divide it between us," said his young friend.

"No, that is not the right thing to do. We can locate the owner with the identification card," answered the older boy.

"You are a fool. You can try to find the owner by yourself," said the young friend.

After that day, the boys no longer traveled together.

The older boy who found the wallet returned it to the owner, who rewarded him with one hundred dollars. He brought the money home and told his parents how he had earned it. His parents praised him and advised him to open a savings account. This made the boy very happy.

---

## MORAL

*Before making friends with others, be sure they are honest and sincere in character.*

# TWO BROTHERS AND THE
# STOLEN COINS

One morning, a family of four—two boys who were eight and ten years old, respectively, and their father and mother—sat down at the dining table for breakfast.

The father blessed the meal and, as they started eating, the eight-year-old said, "Dad, someone has been stealing my coins from the jar I use to save my money."

The father responded, "Maybe you miscounted, son. Count it again; I'm certain it is all there."

"But Daddy," the youth said, "I always put coins in the jar and, instead of it filling up, the amount seems to get less and less." Pointing at his brother, he added, "Besides Dad, you know that only the two of us use the room."

"Did you take any coins out of your brother's jar?" the father asked the older brother.

"No, I did not," the ten-year-old boy replied.

That evening, as the mother prepared dinner and the father helped the younger son with his homework, they heard a crashing sound upstairs.

"What's that?" the father yelled, loud enough for the older boy to hear.

There was no response. The father sent his younger son upstairs to see what had happened.

The boy returned, crying. "The jar with my coins is broken and the coins are all over the floor," the boy told his father, as tears streamed down his cheeks.

"Come downstairs, now!" the father called out to his older son.

"What happened upstairs?" his father asked, as the boy walked slowly down the stairs.

"I was just checking to see how many coins he had," the older son answered.

"I will not accept that answer," the father said. "I need you to tell me the truth. No more lies. Did you or did you not take your brother's coins from the jar?"

The boy looked at his younger brother and his mother, and then looked at his father. With his head bowed to avoid looking into his father's eyes, he replied, "Yes, I did, and I am very sorry."

"How could you steal, and from your own brother?" his mother interjected.

"It is wrong to steal. It doesn't matter whether it is from your brother or a stranger; it is stealing. Son, to make matters worse, you lied to me about it. Why are you taking his money, anyway? You have your own allowance!" the father said.

"My allowance is not enough. When I go to the candy store with my friends, they always have more money than me. That is why I took his money," the older brother said.

"You cannot compare what you get to what your friends get. Parents give allowances based on what they can afford. I give you what I can afford. You have to learn to be satisfied with what you have. You are grounded for one month. You cannot go out to play after school or have any friends visit you. During that time, also, your brother will be given your allowance, to make up for what you took from him," the father said.

Turning to his younger son, the father said, "Your mother will get you a new jar for your coins. Here is your first dollar." He gave him four shiny, new quarters.

The young boy smiled and said, "Thanks, Dad!"

---

## **MORAL**

*Children should be trained to live with both little and plenty. It minimizes future problems.*

---

# THE FATHER AND HIS TWO SONS

**A** man had two sons. One was fifteen years old and the other sixteen.

The fifteen-year-old son pretended to be deaf to get his father's attention. Each time his father called his name or asked him to perform a task, he pretended he did not hear him. The father had to repeat the request or touch him to get his attention.

The father told the boy's teacher about his behavior.

The teacher said his behavior was normal in school. She added that she noticed no change in his hearing and she never had to repeat her instructions to him.

The father took his son to the doctor for a hearing test, which proved that he had no hearing impairment.

The father expressed his love to both sons and pleaded with his younger son to stop pretending he was deaf.

One summer day, the father and the boys went hunting in the forest. The boys were walking ahead of the father, about forty or fifty yards, and approximately ten feet across from each other.

The father looked beyond them and saw a mountain lion, standing on a ledge, poised to attack the boys. The father yelled out to the boys to get down, while he positioned his rifle.

The older son immediately dropped to the ground, but the younger son looked around and yelled, "What did you say?"

The lion attacked the younger boy, as the father shot the lion. It fell to the ground, close to the boy, who was bleeding profusely from his wounds.

When the boy healed, he promised his father he would always listen carefully to what he had to say, and always follow his instructions.

## **MORAL**

*Pretending to be what you are not can back fire on you.*

KENNETH E. POLLOCK

# A BASKET OF GOLD

**A** master said to two of his most loyal servants, "Today is your lucky day! I made you a promise five years ago, which I am about to keep. You are both free to go anywhere you choose," he said. "I will give you the legal documents you need for traveling."

He took them to the barn and showed them a pile of dried corn and a pile of rich topsoil that had yielded good crops. The master's property was known for having good topsoil.

"You can share these in whatever way you choose," the master said, pointing to the piles.

After some discussion, the younger man decided to take the corn for himself and offered the topsoil to the older man. "I can eat my corn when I am hungry," he said. "I do not have time to wait for the topsoil to fertilize the seeds so they can grow."

The older man responded, "We can divide the corn and the topsoil between us."

But the younger man insisted on keeping all the corn for himself.

The men thanked their master for keeping his word and said goodbye to him.

The younger man loaded the corn in a basket and placed it on his head, balancing it with both hands.

The older man put the topsoil in a basket lined with plastic and placed it on his shoulders, balancing it with one hand.

In this manner, they started on their journey to a new life of freedom.

About a mile into their journey, it started to rain. The corn in the younger man's basket became soaked from the rain. He decided that his load was too heavy, so he dumped out the corn.

The soil in the older man's basket started to overflow. As the soil flowed from the basket, it was replaced with rain water. When the rain stopped, the older man took the basket from his shoulders and

placed it on the ground. When he looked into the basket, he saw several small stones on the bottom of the basket. He reached into the basket to remove the stones and, as he did so, the soil, which was still clinging to them, washed away to reveal bright golden nuggets. He looked up into the sky at the bright sun, which was shining again and thanked his Creator for his good fortune.

The younger man became excited when he saw the gold nuggets and asked the older man to share them with him.

The older man refused, saying, "If you had not been so selfish, we would both have gold and corn. But you were selfish; you took all the corn for yourself, and when it became too heavy for you to transport, you dumped it on the master's property, and so gave it back to him. By refusing to share with me, you lost the opportunity to share my gold."

---

### **<u>MORAL</u>**

*When you share with others in good times, your chances are greater that they will be supportive of you in troubled times.*

---

## ABOUT THE AUTHOR

KENNETH E. POLLOCK is an African-American, born in the island of St. Kitts, the sister isle of Nevis, in the Caribbean.

Author, motivational speaker and humanitarian, this successful entrepreneur holds among his many concerns the direction of the youth of the world. He is also an advocate for the homeless, victims of AIDS and undocumented residents in the U.S.A.

As a freelance writer, Mr. Pollock has written various newspaper and magazine articles on social issues that impact the lives of African-Americans. His activities have been featured in the New York Daily News, New York Newsday, Carib News, Class Magazine, Everybody's Magazine and the Daily Challenge.

An avid reader, as illustrated by this book, Mr. Pollock is a student of Aesop, the master of fables.

Mr. Pollock immigrated to the United States in 1967. He is a U.S. Army Vietnam era veteran who resides in New York City with his wife Yvonne Humphrey-Pollock. He is the father of two sons and two daughters from a previous marriage.

# MOTIVATIONAL POSTERS/BOOKS

**Each poster includes a moral and the full or abbreviated story. Order individual poster by the title of the story; each poster costs $5.00 plus shipping and handling. Purchase 5 posters and pay only $20.00 plus shipping and handling. Poster size 22" x 14".**

Name_____

Mailing Address _____

City_____State_____Zip_____

Title_____Title_____

Title_____Title_____

## DISCOUNT AND WHOLESALE RATES FOR NONPROFIT ORGANIZATIONS, SCHOOLS, CHURCHES AND BUSINESSES
### Posters:
Number of Posters @ US$5.00 each - Total_____
### Books:
**Philosophy of Life-Stories for Young People**
Volume One @ US $12.95_____ Canadian $15.95_____
### (Plus shipping and handling)

Telephone #:_____

Fax #: _____

E-mail Address:_____

## Payment Information
Credit Card # _____ Exp. Date_____

Card Holder's Name _____

Cardholder's Signature_____

Purchase Amount_____ Purchase Date _____

**Payment by check:**
Check # _____Routing_____

Check dated_____Check Amount _____

Isis Publishing House, Ltd.
4620 Kings Highway, P.O. Box 340487
Brooklyn, New York 11234
Telephone: (212) 882-1018 or (718) 253-9387
Fax: (718) 253-2699
E-mail: isispublishingco@aol.com
Website: www.isispublishingusa.com